Little Blue Truck Farm Sticker Fun!

Written by

Alice Schertle

Illustrated by

Jill McElmurry

HOUGHTON MIFFLIN HARCOURT
BOSTON NEW YORK 2013

Text copyright © 2013 by Alice Schertle. Illustrations copyright © 2013 by Jill McElmurry. This book is based on the following: *Little Blue Truck* text copyright © 2006 by Alice Schertle. Illustrations copyright © 2006 by Jill McElmurry. *Little Blue Truck Leads the Way* text copyright © 2009 by Alice Schertle. Illustrations copyright © 2009 by Jill McElmurry. All rights reserved. HMH Books is an imprint of Houghton Mifflin Harcourt Publishing Company, 222 Berkeley Street, Boston, Massachusetts 02116.

ISBN 978-0-544-06687-8

Design by Carol Chu

www.hmhbooks.com

Manufactured in China | SCP 10 9 8 7 6 5 4 3 2 1 | 4500409302

Beep! Beep! Here comes Blue! He's a friendly little truck with big-rig pluck.
In the fall, leaves turn red, orange, and yellow, but Blue is always blue.
Can you make Blue his own special color?

The leaves are starting to fall off the trees. Count how many leaves are still on the tree. How many are on the ground?

____ leaves on the tree

____ leaves on the ground

The Fall Festival is coming up and Blue needs to deliver some pumpkins to the mayor. Can you help him find his way into the city?

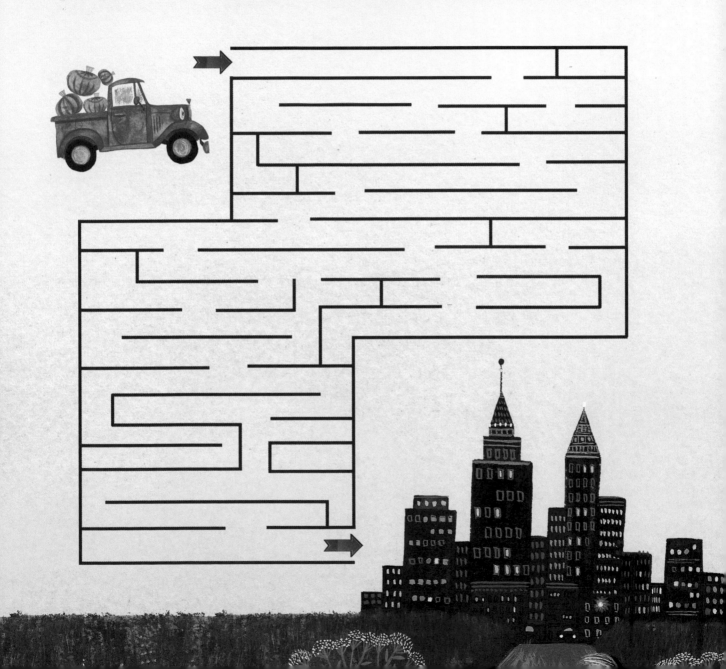

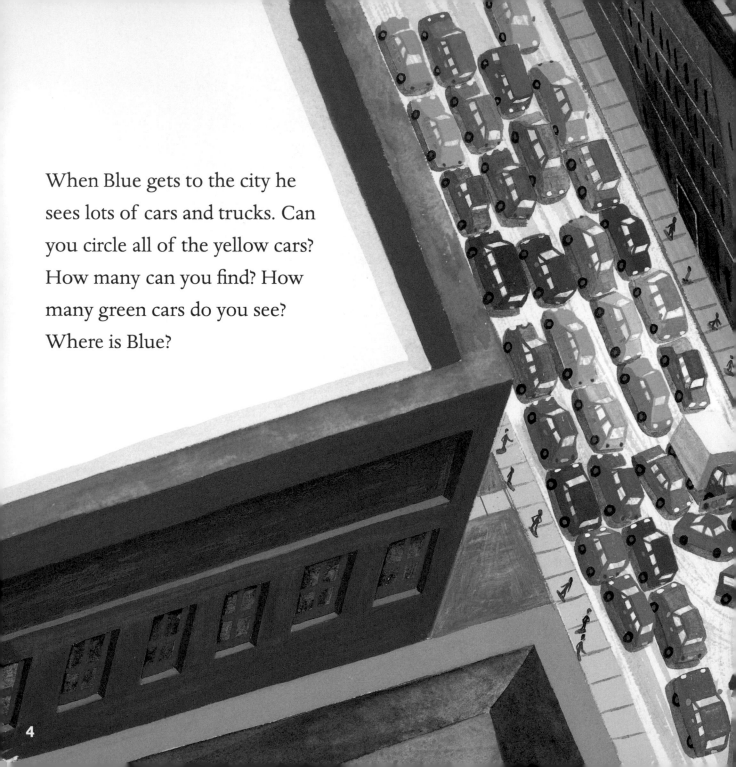

When Blue gets to the city he sees lots of cars and trucks. Can you circle all of the yellow cars? How many can you find? How many green cars do you see? Where is Blue?

_____ yellow cars

_____ green cars

5

The mayor is hosting a pumpkin decorating contest with all the pumpkins Blue delivered. You can make fancy pumpkins, too! Draw a face or special design on each pumpkin.

Blue is driving the mayor in the Fall Festival parade and he needs to wear a fancy banner. Use your stickers and some crayons to help Blue decorate his banner and make it special.

On the way back from the city, Little Blue picks up his animal friends. They make a lot of noise! Use your stickers to show what sound each animal makes. Place each sound sticker in the correct speech bubble. What noise does Blue make?

Blue and his friends are off to the
orchard. They want ripe autumn apples
for apple pies! There are red apples,
green apples, and yellow ones, too.
Blue thinks crisp green apples make the
best pies. Help Blue by circling all the
green apples you can see. How many
can you find? _____ green apples

Mmm mmm! Apple pie! Pumpkin pie! Two of the best things about fall! Look at all the different pies. Can you find two that are the same? Circle the pie that looks most delicious to you. What kind of pie do you think it is?

1

2

3

4

5

6

Fall is harvest time on the farm. Blue is loading his truck bed with yummy fall foods to deliver to the farmer's market. Use your stickers to help fill Little Blue with apples, pumpkins, squash, and corn!

What yummy foods Blue and his friends found at the farm! Can you help them add up the fruits and vegetables they gathered?

+ = _____apples

+ = _____ pumpkins

+ = _____squash

+ = _____ears of corn

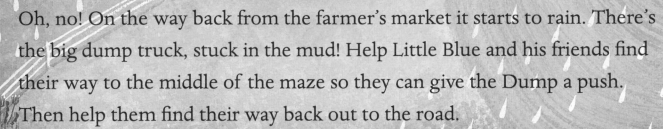

Oh, no! On the way back from the farmer's market it starts to rain. There's the big dump truck, stuck in the mud! Help Little Blue and his friends find their way to the middle of the maze so they can give the Dump a push. Then help them find their way back out to the road.

There are so many things Blue loves about fall!
Look for all of Blue's favorite fall words and circle them in the word
search. Words can go down, across, or diagonally.

apple

costumes

pie

pumpkin

crisp

farm

corn

leaves

```
P U M P K I N S
C O R N C Y E L
T B U O O M R E
F A R F U T C A
A N P T A V R V
R Z S P O P I E
M O K Z L I S S
C J S E U E P Z
```

Now draw a picture of yourself enjoying a favorite fall activity!
Use your stickers to help decorate your picture.

Blue and his friends are going to decorate
the barn for a costume party! Use your
stickers to help them get the barn ready,
and then use crayons or colored pencils to
draw an autumn sky!

Now that the barn is ready for the party, it's time to get dressed up!
Blue needs a costume. What should he be? Use your imagination and draw
a costume on Blue. Will you give him a hat? A mustache? A bow tie?

All Blue's friends have their costumes on, too. Can you guess what they are? Use the words in the box to figure out each animal's costume and write it on the line below.

clown
ghost
witch
sailor
pirate
prince
cowboy

_____

_____

_____

What a fun fall day this has been! But now it's time for Little Blue to head home and let his engine rest. Can you help Blue find the road that leads back to his warm, snug garage?